In memory of Jason - C.F.
For my own biscuit bandit, Harry - M.B.

First published 2019 by Macmillan Children's Books
an imprint of Pan Macmillan,
The Smithson, 6 Briset Street, London EC1M 5NR
EU representative: Macmillan Publishers Ireland Ltd, 1st Floor,
The Liffey Trust Centre, 117–126 Sheriff Street Upper
Dublin 1, D01 YC43
Associated companies throughout the world
www.panmacmillan.com

ISBN: 978-1-5098-8240-3

Text copyright © Claire Freedman 2019
Illustrations copyright © Mike Byrne 2019

3 5 7 9 8 6 4 2

A CIP catalogue record for this book is
available from the British Library.

Printed in China.

DUCKTECTIVE QUACK

AND THE CAKE CRIME WAVE

Written by
CLAIRE FREEDMAN

Illustrated by
MIKE BYRNE

MACMILLAN CHILDREN'S BOOKS

At the police station, Ducktective Quack,
Had the most puzzling crime wave to crack.
A thief was at large, but what was at stake?
The town's favourite food . . .

. . . this robber
stole
cake!

Ducktective Quack called to Constable Crackling,
"Fetch me our files, this case needs our tackling.
We must catch the thief. Quick! They have to be beaten,
Before all the cakes in our town have been eaten!"

Just then the phone rang - a call from Miss Sweet,
Who owned Cream Puffs cake shop, the best in the street.
"I just turned my back and I've had such a shock,
Someone has stolen my chocolate cake stock!"

"Quick, Crackling!" said Quack.
"Let's not waste any time.
We must hurry at once
to the scene of the crime!"

But at Cream Puffs they only found leftover crumbs
And chocolatey smudges from fingers and thumbs.
"Who's been in your shop?" questioned Quack with a frown.
Miss Sweet mentioned names, and Quack jotted them down.

"Ho-hum!" said 'Tec Quack. "and that's ALL you've seen?"
"Well my mail is here," Miss Sweet said, "so the postman has been."

Reader, are you looking
And noting down clues?
We must catch the villain,
There's no time to lose!

Back at the station, Quack told Crackling, "Look,
At the long list of suspects I wrote in my book!"
There was old Mr Gummy, the dentist next door,
Fred Bear and the Cat Twins, would they break the law?

Now, who had a motive? Who liked cake a lot?
Most people! So that narrowed down the list . . . NOT!

POLICE DEPARTMENT
FRED BEAR
1010 09

POLICE DEPARTMENT
DR GUMMY M.D
300179

LICE DEPARTMENT
RONI CAT
30914

POLICE DEPARTMENT
REG CAT
040716

Hmm, so many suspects
And all with one link,
They came to the shop,
But what do YOU think?

Just then Postman Pete arrived late with the mail,
He normally delivered by ten without fail.
"Did you see any strangers at Cream Puffs?" Quack said.
"I didn't!" cried Pete, and with that off he sped.

"Let's see our first suspect," said Quack, "Mr Gummy.
Perhaps he's our thief, chocolate cake is so yummy."

They saw Mr Gummy to give him a grilling,
But when they arrived he was doing a filling.

"It can't have been me," Gummy said with relief. "I never eat cakes, they are bad for your teeth!"

Do you think Mr Gummy Is telling the truth, Or is he to blame? YOU are the sleuth!

Next task on their list was to question Fred Bear,
The town's finest tailor, who made things to wear.
"What me? I'm no cake thief!" Fred said with a grin.
Although I like cake, I prefer to stay slim!"

That left just the Cat Twins,
who said, "Wasn't us!
We only bought bread,
then went home on the bus.

Fred Bear looks suspicious.
Although he is slim,
Perhaps he eats cake
And then goes to the gym?

The very next day, at the new Doughnut Bar,
Some doughnuts went missing and caused a hoo-ha.
Nobody noticed, so no one saw who
Could commit such a crime without leaving a clue.

Have you noticed the clues?
What is your belief?
Did you spot anybody
Who might be the thief?

At the police station, Ducktective Quack
Suddenly put down her files with a thwack!
"We've been through the suspects and none of them fit,
But someone is missing
                              - oh,

I'm such a
                    twit!"

"A cake-eating thief will be putting on weight,
Their thieving might cause them to always be late.

Paw Print

CAKE CRIME WAVE

And eating up buns oozing sugary fillings
Is so bad for teeth, they might need dental drillings."

There's only one person who fits the description
Quack knew who it was, she had a conviction!

"I've cracked this tough case!" Quack announced with a boast,
"And here they come now . . ."

Can you solve the puzzle?
It's easy to see
Who exactly the thief is,
But do you agree?

"...they're bringing the post!"

The postman confessed. "Yes, it's true. It was me!
I just can't resist cakes and doughnuts, you see.
I know it was wrong. I was going to stop.
If I gobble more cake, I think I'll go POP!"

"Worse still, all that cake that I ate and I ate
Was bad for my teeth and so bad for my weight!"

WANTED
HAVE YOU SEEN THIS BEAR?
KEV KOALA
17891146
POLICE DEP
1-800-WANTED

Did you solve the crime?
Did you spot every clue?
For if you did – brilliant!
Well done to you!

Pete promised to pay back the money he owed.
Quack said, "No more cakes for you, or you'll explode!
As this is your first crime, we'll let you go free."
"I'll be good from now on," said Pete. "Wait and see!"

The cake crime wave ended
that very same day.
When the town heard the news
they cheered hip, hip, hooray!
"Let's celebrate!" said Quack.
"Let's both have a slice
Of carrot cake, Crackling.
It's healthy and nice!"

NO CAKE

So now if the town
Has a new crime to crack,
Do offer to help out
Our Ducktective Quack!

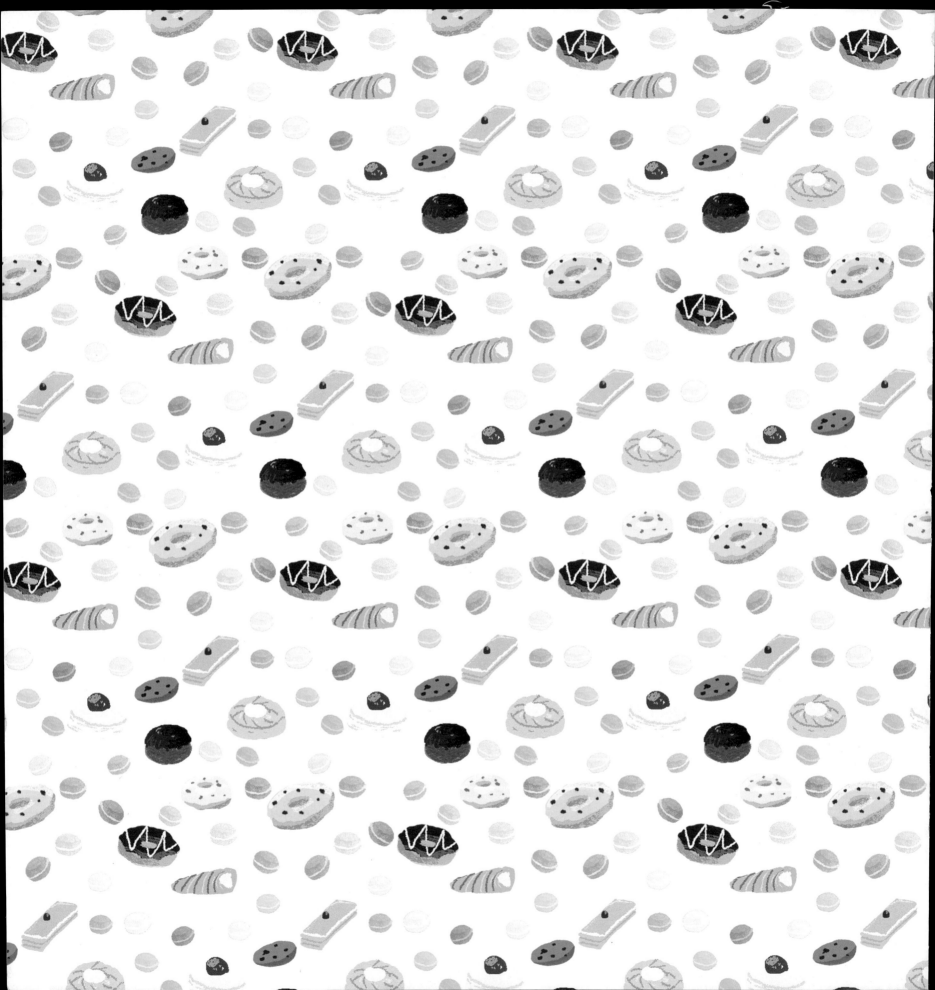